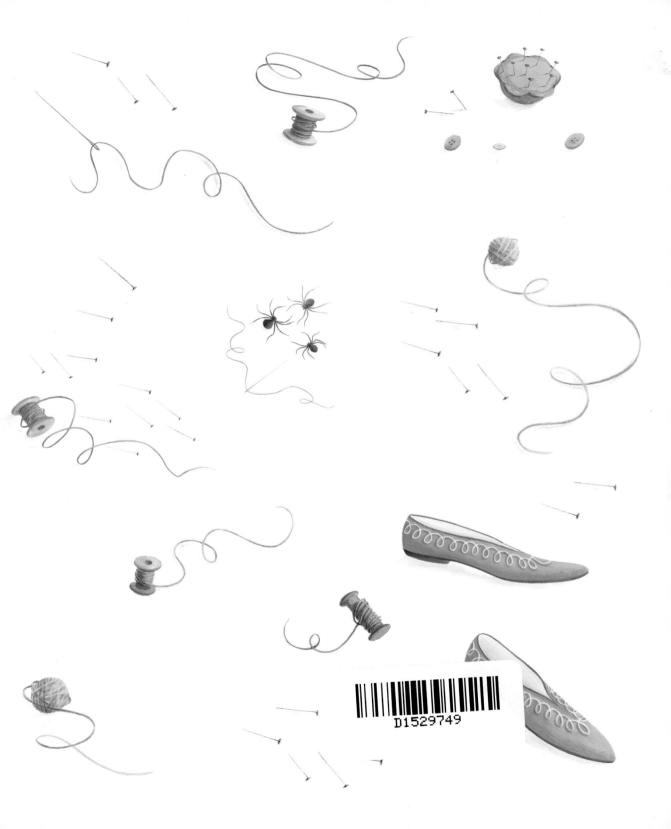

D1529749

For my god daughter, Flora — *KP*

For Boris and Rob — *MCS*

First published in 2003 by Orion Children's Books
a division of the Orion Publishing Group Ltd
Orion House
5 Upper St Martin's Lane
London WC2H 9EA

Text copyright © Kate Petty 2003
Illustrations copyright © Mary Claire Smith 2003
Designed by Sarah Hodder

A catalogue record for this book is available from the British Library
Printed and bound in Italy
ISBN 1 85881 836 2

The Nightspinners

Kate Petty

illustrated by Mary Claire Smith

Orion
Children's Books

There was once a girl who lived in a house in the woods. Her name
was Ariane, and though she spent the days by herself she was never
lonely. All the animals – rabbits and squirrels, deer and foxes – were her
friends. Ariane even liked the beetles and woodlice that scuttled across
her floor, and she loved to watch spiders spin their gleaming threads.
She never brushed away the shining new webs that were their homes.

Ariane was a weaver too. She sat at
her loom all day weaving cotton
and silk and wool.

When she wove wool, she
thought of sheep in fields, of
green grass and purple heather.

When she wove cotton, she
imagined soft white clouds against
the bright blue sky.

When she wove silk, she
thought of silkworms spinning
their cocoons, never knowing
that one day they would be
turned into clothes for kings
and queens.

Everyone nearby knew what a clever
weaver Ariane was. She worked hard and
she was happy in her house in the woods.

Then one day everything changed.

Queen Heartless went to the Springtime Ball and saw a princess wearing a beautiful ballgown made of the finest silk. It was even finer than her own.

Queen Heartless was angry. She frowned and clenched her fists. "Bring me the person who wove that fine silk!" she hissed. "They shall make cloth for no one but me!"

Next morning a messenger rode to Ariane's house. She was sitting outside, eating bread and cheese with herbs from the garden, and feeding crumbs to the birds.

"You must come with me," said the messenger. "Queen Heartless orders you to weave for no one but her."

"But I don't want to," said Ariane. "I'm happy here. I don't want to leave my home or my friends, the animals. Besides, I work for whom I please."

The messenger saw the sense in this and rode back to tell Queen Heartless what Ariane had said.

Queen Heartless was really angry.

"Bring me this ungrateful girl or I'll chop off your head," she cried.

Again the messenger rode through the woods to Ariane's house. "I'll surprise her and tie her up," he thought. "Then she'll have to come."

He hid in the trees until he saw Ariane hard at work. Then he burst into her house. He grabbed her so roughly that he broke the threads she was weaving and smashed her precious loom to splinters.

He held her tight and tied her up. Then he threw her onto his horse and galloped back to the palace.

"So!" said Queen Heartless, when poor Ariane was brought to her. "You are the girl that defies me! For that you shall set to work straight away. Here is a loom. Here are reels of blue silk thread. Weave me silk for a dress that will look like the evening sky just after the sun has gone down."

Ariane set up the loom and started to weave.
She wove all night and by morning she had
made a length of silk that glowed as richly
as the evening sky, just after the sun
has gone down.

A maid bought her bread and water for breakfast.

"I have eaten nothing since yesterday," said Ariane. "And I have worked all night. I need more than this."

When Queen Heartless heard that Ariane had dared to complain, she said, "I command her to weave me more silk, for a ballgown that will look like a field of waving corn. Give her these reels of golden thread and tell her she shall have no more food until the cloth is ready."

So Ariane had to sit at the loom and weave. She wove beautiful cloth that rippled like a field of golden corn waving in the wind, while tears ran down her face and dropped on to the gorgeous silken folds.

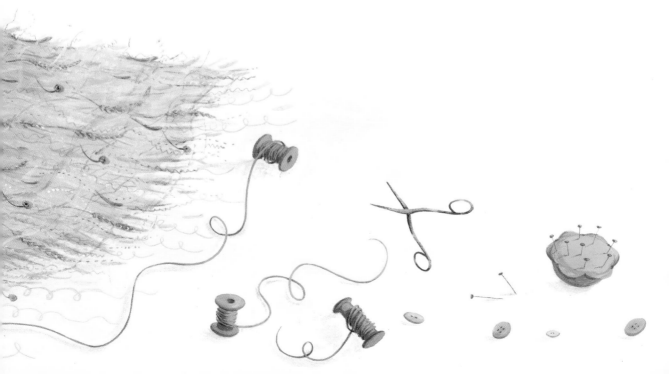

Next morning Queen Heartless came to fetch the golden cloth herself. Her eyes lit up when she saw it, but she didn't thank Ariane. She simply snatched the silk and marched off, locking the door behind her.

Ariane was so tired and hungry. She longed to be back in her house with her animal friends. She rattled the handle of the locked door. "Let me out!" she shouted. "How can I work if I have nothing to eat or drink?"

When Queen Heartless heard all the noise she was angrier than ever. "You shall have bread and water to keep you alive," she said, "but now I want a ballgown that shimmers like the morning dew. In fact, I want it while the dew is still on the grass. You had better start now!"

"How can I, when I have no thread?" asked Ariane.

"I don't know," said Queen Heartless spitefully, "but if I don't have silk that glistens like the morning dew by dawn tomorrow, I will chop off your head."

Ariane sat down and cried herself to sleep.

She was woken by a tiny voice calling her name. "Ariane!" it said. "Ariane, talk to me."

Ariane looked all around, but the room was empty. She saw something move and looked closer. What should she see but a spider!

"Ariane," said the spider. "I can help you if you'll let me."

"That's very kind of you," said Ariane, who was used to talking to animals. "But no one can help me now. I'm too tired to weave any more, and anyway, I have no thread."

"Sleep, Ariane," said the spider. "I promise you there will be enough silk for a ballgown when you wake. Trust me!"

Even if the spider had not spoken,
Ariane would have fallen asleep again.
Nothing could save her — certainly not
one little spider. Why, it would take a
thousand spiders to weave enough silk
for a ballgown!

The spider looked at Ariane as she slept. Then it ran to find two friends. "We must save Ariane," said the spider. "I am going to weave a fine silk square. I want you to do the same and bring them to me in this corner of the room as fast as you can, but not before you have both asked two more friends to do exactly the same."

The two spiders scuttled off, eager to help. Meanwhile, the first spider sat down to spin her own silk and weave a fine web, the size of a tiny lace handkerchief. When it was finished it was just the silvery, misty colour of dew on the grass as dawn breaks.

Before long, the spider's two friends brought her their work, so there were three pieces of silk. Very soon after, four more spiders came along with four more pieces of silk. Then eight spiders brought another eight fine webs.

As the night wore on, sixteen more spiders arrived and then another thirty-two, sixty-four, one hundred and twenty-eight, two hundred and fifty-six… The first spider ran to and fro showing the others how to fasten their webs of silk together into a single length.

When Ariane woke up she thought she must still be dreaming. Before her eyes the most beautiful piece of silk seemed to be weaving itself. Five hundred and eleven wonderfully woven pieces were being made into one, and as she watched, five hundred and twelve more spiders scuttled under the door, each with their square of silk. The spiders laid the squares down so the cloth was ten squares across and one hundred squares long, with a few left over.

They spun and wove, spun and wove, until all the pieces were made into one piece of silk that shimmered like the morning dew. It was exactly one metre wide and ten metres long, just right for a beautiful ballgown.

As the sun rose, Ariane saw the door open. Her blood froze. There stood Queen Heartless, with a soldier dressed all in black at her side.

"Your silk is ready," said Ariane as calmly as she could. But Queen Heartless did not see the silk. All she saw were one thousand and twenty-three spiders. She screamed, but the spiders were on her as she fell to the floor. They ran all over her.

"Help me!" she screamed. But the soldier had fled, and so had Ariane, the roll of magical silk tucked under her arm.

Ariane ran and ran and ran, back through the woods to her house.

Next day a prince rode through the woods. When he saw the spider-spun silk through the window he knew that here was something rare indeed. He knocked on the door to find out who had woven it.

He couldn't believe his eyes when a beautiful girl opened the door. He paid for the silk and said he would come back next week for more, because he wanted an excuse to see Ariane again.

Ariane mended her loom. The prince visits her often and one day she might marry him, but for now she is happy with her animal friends, working for whom she pleases.

If you look hard, you might see more cobwebs than usual around the house and garden. They sparkle in the sunlight, just like the morning dew.

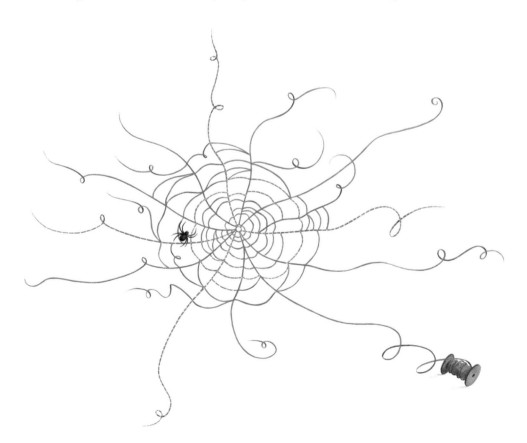

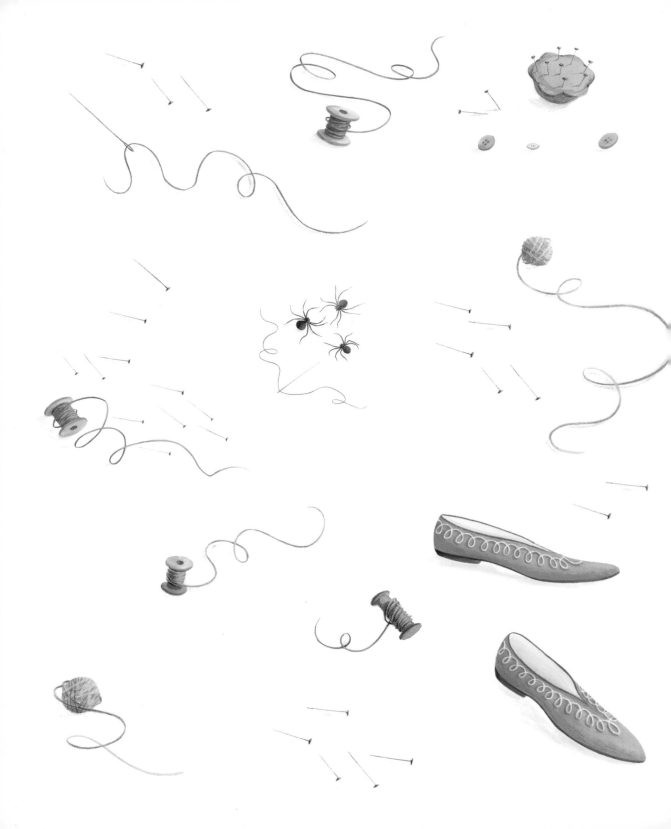